W9-ACH-899
09/2017

DISCARD

An I Can Read Book®

# The Adventures of Snail at School

## Story and pictures by
## John Stadler

HarperTrophy®
*A Division of HarperCollinsPublishers*

*To the children of*
*Enfield Elementary School,*
*Enfield, New Hampshire*

HarperCollins®, 🏠®, Harper Trophy®, and I Can Read Book®
are trademarks of HarperCollins Publishers.

The Adventures of Snail at School
Copyright © 1993 by John Stadler
Printed in the United States of America. All rights reserved.
For information address HarperCollins Children's Books, a division
of HarperCollins Publishers, 195 Broadway, New York, NY 10007.

❖

Library of Congress Cataloging-in-Publication Data
Stadler, John.
   The adventures of Snail at school / story and pictures by John Stadler.
      p.      cm. — (An I can read book)
   Summary: Snail goes on three errands for his teacher and has amazing adventures.
   ISBN 0-06-021041-9 — ISBN 0-06-021042-7 (lib. bdg.)
   ISBN 0-06-444202-0 (pbk.)
   [1. Snails—Fiction.   2. Schools—Fiction.]   I. Title.
PZ7.S77575Ad   1993                                                91-45403
[E]—dc20                                                              CIP
                                                                       AC

16  17  18   PC/WOR   30  2 9 28  27  26  25  24  23  22

# Contents

# Books for Class

"It is story time, class!"

said Mrs. Harvey.

"Would someone go to the library

and pick up our books

from Mr. Moody?"

"I will," said Snail.

"All right, Snail,"

said Mrs. Harvey.

"Hurry back!"

5

Snail went out the door

and down the long hallway.

He saw a water fountain.

"I am in a hurry," Snail said,

"but I am thirsty too."

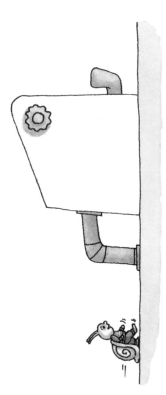

Snail climbed up.

He turned the handle.

*Whoosh!*

Water came rushing out.

"Whoa!" said Snail.

He tumbled.

Snail splashed.

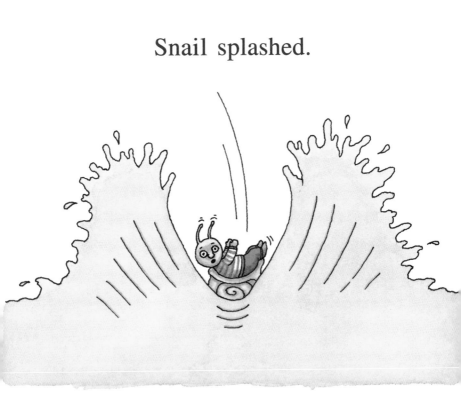

Snail swam.

# Snail rested.

# Snail surfed.

"Here is the library!" cried Snail.

"Those must be our books!"

Snail found the water fountain

and turned the handle.

All the water drained away.

"There you are, Snail,"
said Mrs. Harvey.
"We were wondering
what happened to you."

16

"I took a drink of water,"

said Snail,

"and the ocean came out,

and I was lost and . . ."

"Now, Snail," said Mrs. Harvey,

"do not make up such wild stories.

Please go back to your seat."

Mrs. Harvey picked up the books

and placed them on her table.

"Hmmm," she said to herself.

"I wonder how these books

got so wet."

"Snail?" Mrs. Harvey asked.

"Yes, Mrs. Harvey," said Snail.

"Oh, never mind, Snail,"

Mrs. Harvey said.

"Never mind."

18

# The New Student

"Class, we will have

a new student today,"

said Mrs. Harvey.

"Will someone pick her up

from the principal's office?"

"I can do it," said Snail.

"Well, all right, Snail,"

said Mrs. Harvey.

"But this time please hurry."

"I will be back in a flash,"

said Snail.

Snail hurried down the long hallway.

"I will show Mrs. Harvey

she can count on me," he said.

Snail came to the principal's office.

There was a fire extinguisher

by the door.

"This should not be here,"

he said.

"I will put it back."

Snail pushed.

Suddenly he heard

*Hissss!*

He grabbed the fire extinguisher.

It started to shake, rattle, and roll.

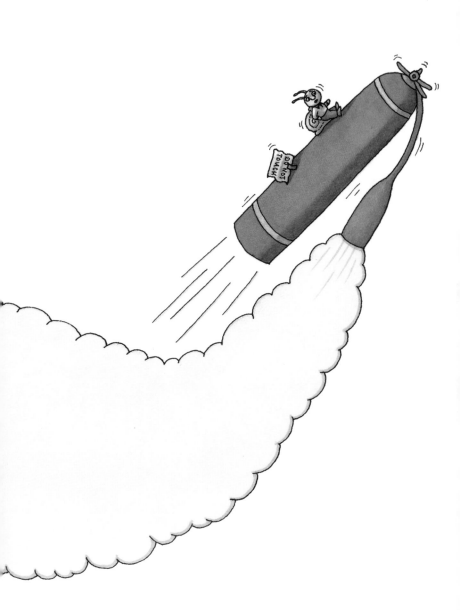

"Yikes!" Snail cried.

"It's blasting off!"

25

"Look at me!

I am in outer space,"

Snail shouted.

Snail landed on another planet.

"Is anybody home?" Snail called.

Suddenly he saw something move.

"Monsters!" cried Snail.

Then he looked closer.

"You are not monsters," said Snail.

"You look like me!"

"Welcome to our planet,"

said one of them.

"My name is Edie."

"Come and join our party,"

said Edie.

"Nice cake," said Snail.

30

"Have a piece," said Edie.

"Thank you very much," Snail said,

"but I must get back

to my classroom."

31

"I can take you
in our rocket,"
said Edie.
"Great!" said Snail.

Edie and Snail

took off for Earth.

"This is my school," said Snail.

"We must hurry.

Mrs. Harvey is waiting for us."

35

"Snail, where have you been?"

asked Mrs. Harvey.

"You could have gone

around the world

in the time you were away!"

"Well," said Snail,

"the fire extinguisher took off,

and I went into space and . . ."

"Now, Snail, please sit down,"

Mrs. Harvey said,

"and stop making up stories."

Mrs. Harvey looked at Edie.
"You must be the new student,"
she said.

"Her name is Edie," said Snail.

"She comes from another planet."

"That is enough, Snail,"

said Mrs. Harvey.

"Welcome to the class, Edie.

You may take your seat

next to Snail."

Then Mrs. Harvey looked closer.

"Edie is floating!"

she said to herself.

"Snail?" Mrs. Harvey asked.

"Yes, Mrs. Harvey," said Snail.

"Oh, never mind, Snail,"

said Mrs. Harvey.

"Never mind."

# Music Lesson

"Who will go

to the music room for me?"

asked Mrs. Harvey.

"I will," Snail said.

"This time I will be quick!"

"Would anyone else like to go?"
asked Mrs. Harvey.
No one moved.

"Well, Snail, it's up to you again,"

said Mrs. Harvey.

"Please tell Miss Pink

that we are ready

for our music lesson,

and ask her to bring

the instruments.

And, Snail," said Mrs. Harvey,

"do not get lost,

and do not come back

with some silly story."

"Don't worry, Mrs. Harvey,"

Snail said.

"I will come right back."

Snail hurried to the music room.
"I wonder where Miss Pink is,"
he said.

Snail waited and waited.

Finally Snail said,

"I cannot wait any longer.

I told Mrs. Harvey

I would hurry.

I will bring the instruments myself."

Snail tried to lift the drum,

but it was too heavy.

49

"What should I do now?"

Snail asked.

Snail sat down

and picked up a baton.

He tapped the floor with it.

*"Ding, ding,"*

rang the triangle.

Snail pointed at the horn.

*"Honk, honk,"*

went the horn.

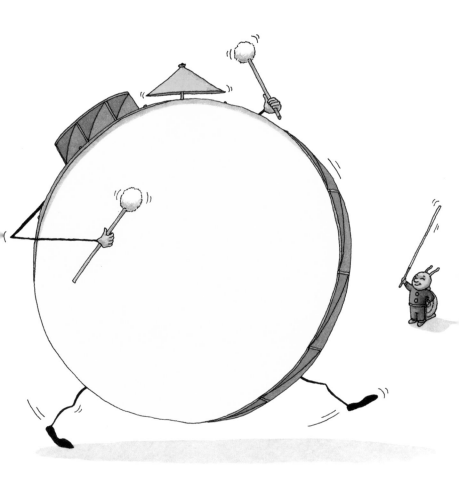

Snail waved the baton

at the drum.

"*Boom, boom,*" went the drum.

Snail was so surprised,

he dropped the baton.

The instruments

ran around the room.

*"Boom! Honk! Ding! Pluck!"*

"Oh, no! What have I done?"

cried Snail.

Then Snail picked up the baton
and waved it.

"Stop!" he yelled.

The instruments stopped running.

"Line up!" ordered Snail.

The instruments lined up.

"To Mrs. Harvey's class!"

Snail shouted.

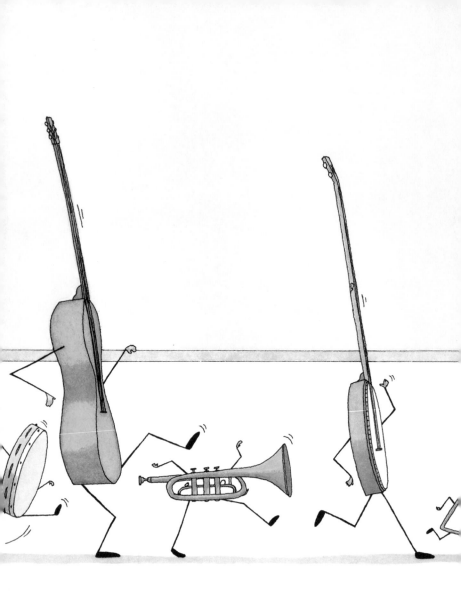

He marched down the hallway.

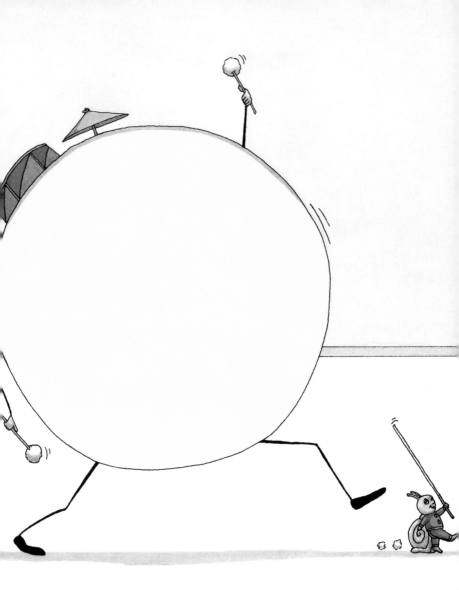

All the instruments followed.

"Stop!" Snail cried,

and he opened the classroom door.

"Finally," said Mrs. Harvey.

"What happened this time, Snail?"

"Miss Pink was not there,"

Snail said,

"and the instruments

ran around and around and . . ."

"Oh, Snail,

I have had enough for today,"

said Mrs. Harvey.

"Please go back to your seat."

61

Just then Miss Pink

rushed into the room.

"I am sorry I am late," she said.

"How did all these instruments

get here?"

"Didn't you bring them?"

asked Mrs. Harvey.

"No, I did not," said Miss Pink.

"Snail," Mrs. Harvey said,

"who really brought them?"

"Well, I picked up the baton,"
said Snail,

"and all the instruments ran . . ."

"Snail," said Mrs. Harvey.

"Yes, Mrs. Harvey," Snail said.

"Never mind, Snail," she said.

"Never mind."